MW00901216

ROSA
DRAWS

FOR you Mum,

because I drew on your Radiator that one time.

First Published in 2018 by words & pictures,
an imprint of The Quarto Group.
6 Orchard Road
Suite 100
Lake Forest, CA 92630
T: +1 949 380 7510
F: +1 949 380 7575
www.QuartoKnows.com

A CIP record for the book is available from the Library of Congress.

ISBN: 978-1-91027-750-8

9 8 7 6 5 4 3 2 1

Manufactured in Dongguan, China TL012018

ROSA DRAWS

words & pictures

This is Rosa.

Rosa loves to draw.

She likes to imagine
and to let her mind soar.

Rosa draws her friendly,
fuzzy black cat.
The cat is wearing
a RIDONKULOUS hat!

Rosa draws the hat
being eaten by a bear.

The bear has the most
GLAM-U-LICIOUS long hair.

Sitting on the hair
is a plum-tastic moose.

The moose has tea
with a *la-dee-dah* goose.

The teapot is stolen
by a NAUGHTY giraffe!

When he tries to run away,

a zillion ants jam his path.

The ants hitch a ride
to avoid being caught,
but poor little Rosa...

...loses her train of thought.

Plunged into the darkness,
no imagination is found.

Rosa's mind spins
around and around.

Thinking and thinking
but nothing comes to mind.

What's this?

A light switch!
What a
FANTASTICAL
find!

"click"

Back on track,

ideas zoom through Rosa's head.

ALL ABOARD!

Her drawings start to spread...

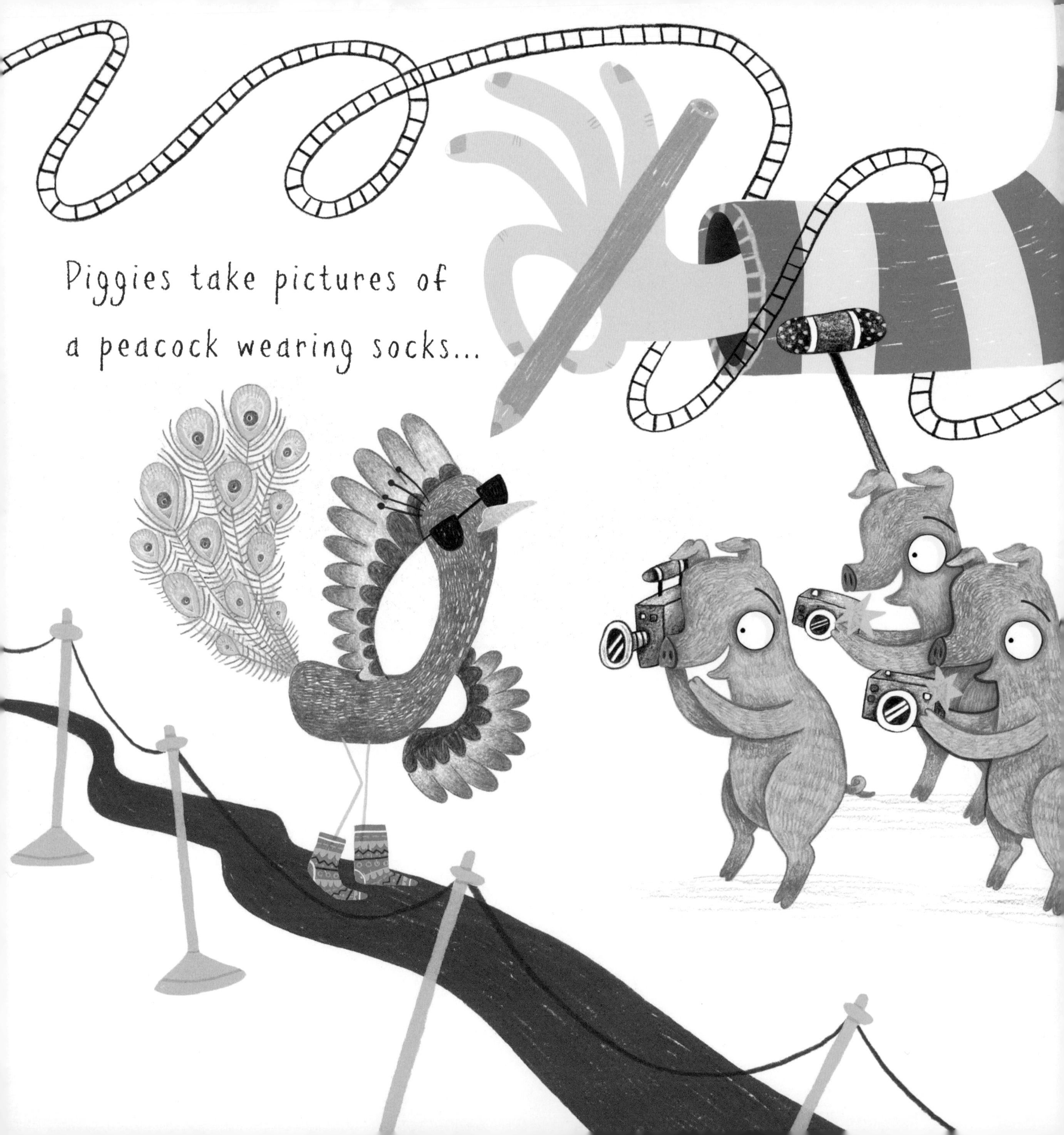

Piggies take pictures of
a peacock wearing socks...

An elephant, a camel, and
a za-za-zoom fox.

HOTEL
THOUGHT
IMAGINATION STATION
la
la

The fox is chased
by an army of bees!
All of the bees
WHIZZ-WHOOSH
on skis.

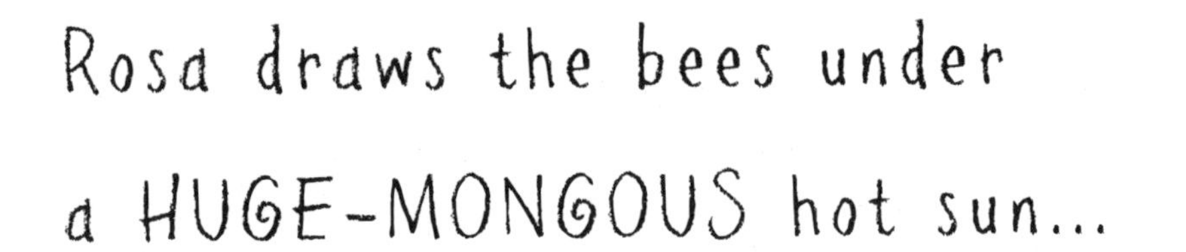

Rosa draws the bees under
a HUGE-MONGOUS hot sun...

"Oh!"

"Oh!"

Rosa says "SORRY!"
for what she has done.

But a moon joins the sun,

colored in blue.

And as it turns out...

...Mom loves to
draw too!